Princess
Mirror-Belle
and the Party Hoppers

★ JULIA DONALDSON ★

Princess Mirror-Belle

and the Party Hoppers

Illustrated by
✳ LYDIA MONKS ✳

MACMILLAN CHILDREN'S BOOKS

These stories first published 2003 in *Princess Mirror-Belle* by
Macmillan Children's Books

This edition published 2015 by Macmillan Children's Books
an imprint of Pan Macmillan
20 New Wharf Road, London N1 9RR
Associated companies throughout the world
www.panmacmillan.com

ISBN 978-1-4472-8489-5

1 3 5 7 9 8 6 4 2

A CIP catalogue record for this book is available from
the British Library.

Printed and bound by CPI Group (UK) Ltd, Croydon CR0 4YY

For Molly

Contents

Chapter One

Party Hoppers

"Happy birthday, Anthony," said Ellen, holding out a present. Her six-year-old cousin snatched it and ripped off the paper.

"It's a book! I hate books—they're boring," he said, throwing it on the floor. "Why couldn't you get me a computer game?"

Anthony was a pain, and the most painful

thing about him was that he was exactly two years younger than Ellen's friend Livvy. Their parties were on the same day, and Mum always insisted that Ellen went to Anthony's one. It just wasn't fair – especially this year, when Livvy's eighth birthday party was in the swimming pool, with inflatables to bounce about on and pizzas in the café afterwards.

"Let's play a few games before tea," said Anthony's mother, Auntie Pam, brightly. Ellen's heart sank even lower. The games were always the same – Stick the Tail on the Donkey, Pass the Parcel and Musical Chairs, and Anthony always won at least two of them – his mother saw to that.

Auntie Pam stuck up a big picture of a donkey without a tail and gave each child a paper tail with their name written on it.

"How about you going first, as you're the oldest, Ellen?" she suggested. She tied a scarf round Ellen's eyes and guided her towards the donkey picture. Ellen pinned the tail on to it blindly and everyone laughed. Auntie Pam removed the scarf and Ellen saw that the tail was sticking on to one of the donkey's ears.

All the other guests had goes, till the donkey had tails growing out of its legs, mane and nose. Then it was Anthony's turn. "Don't tie it too tight!" he ordered his mother. When he was standing in front of the donkey picture Ellen noticed him tilting his head back and she guessed that he was peeping out from below the scarf. Sure enough, he stuck the tail on to exactly the right spot.

"Brilliant, birthday boy!" said Auntie Pam, and presented him with the prize, which was an enormous box of chocolates. "Now let's play Dead Lions," she said. This was a game where you all had to lie on the floor  and try not to move. If you moved you were Out – unless you were Anthony, in which case you squealed, "I didn't move, I didn't move, I *didn't*!" until your mother gave you another chance.

Auntie Pam produced a box of face paints and suggested that for a change the children might like to be different jungle animals – not just lions. She got Ellen to help her paint zebra and tiger stripes on to the younger children's faces, in front of the big mirror in the hall.

The made-up children raced back into the sitting room and Ellen was left to paint her own face. She felt in rather a poisonous mood so she decided to be a snake. She picked up the green stick and was about to start painting her face when she saw the mirror lips move and heard a familiar voice.

"Are you sure you've been invited?" asked Mirror-Belle.

Ellen felt ridiculously glad to see her. It was true that Mirror-Belle usually spelled trouble, but she was much more fun than Anthony and his friends.

"Of course I've been invited. It's my cousin's party," Ellen replied, glancing around to check that no one else could see Mirror-Belle climbing out of the mirror.

Mirror-Belle looked around too. "Oh

dear," she said. "I seem to be in the wrong place. I'm supposed to be at the wood nymphs' party. That was why I was painting my face green." Like Ellen, she had a box of face paints in one hand and a green stick in the other.

"I see you're planning to go green too," she said. "Is your cousin a wood elf or something?"

"No, he's a monster," said Ellen, and she told Mirror-Belle about Anthony and about how she really wanted to go to Livvy's swimming party.

"And so you shall!" said Mirror-Belle, sounding like the Fairy Godmother in *Cinderella*. "Off you go! I'll stay here and pretend to be you."

Ellen felt torn. "But Mirror-Belle . . . I

don't know . . . could you really do that?"

"Of course," replied Mirror-Belle. "I'm an expert at pretending. In fact, I've got several gold medals for it."

Ellen could well believe that; she often wondered how many of Mirror-Belle's stories about herself were true. All the same, she was still worried about leaving her at Anthony's party.

"But you'd have to *behave* like me, not like you," she said. "You'd have to be shy and sensible, and you'd have to promise not to—" but she never finished the sentence because she heard Auntie Pam calling her.

"Coming!" said Mirror-Belle, and strode into the sitting room. There was no choice left. Ellen crept to the front door and let herself out.

The swimming pool wasn't far from Anthony's house. Ellen ran all the way. Livvy and the other guests had only just arrived, and Livvy's mother was giving them all 20p pieces for the lockers.

"Ellen!" shouted Livvy. "That's brilliant – I thought you had to go to your cousin's party. Where are your swimming things?"

"Oh dear. I left them at home," said Ellen. She felt foolish, particularly as she was still clutching the box of face paints.

"Shall I phone your mother and ask her to bring them round?" offered Livvy's mother.

"Er . . . no, she's gone out," said Ellen.

"Well, never mind – I expect you can

borrow a costume and towel from Lost Property," and Livvy's mother went off to organise this.

"Is that my present? I love face paints!" said Livvy.

"Er, yes," said Ellen, thrusting the box into her hands. "I'm sorry I didn't have time to wrap them up." She'd never told Livvy about Mirror-Belle and this didn't seem a good time to start.

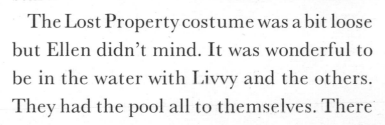

The Lost Property costume was a bit loose but Ellen didn't mind. It was wonderful to be in the water with Livvy and the others. They had the pool all to themselves. There was a huge inflatable sea monster, and a pirate ship and a desert island. Livvy made up a really good game called Sharks, where you had to swim from the desert island to the ship without being caught by a shark. If you got caught you were taken to the sea monster and had to wait on its back to be rescued. Ellen was a fast swimmer and managed to rescue several fishes from the sharks. That was fun, but the best thing about the game was that Anthony wasn't there to cheat and squeal and clamour for a prize. (There weren't any prizes, which was another good thing.)

Ellen was in the middle of a particularly daring rescue when Livvy, who was one of the sharks, grabbed her by the shoulder strap of her costume. Ellen tried to swim

away and the strap snapped.

The swimming-pool attendant beckoned to Ellen. "Pop into the changing area and they'll find you a safety pin," she said.

As Ellen fixed the strap in front of the mirror in the changing area she remembered Mirror-Belle and wondered how she was getting on at Anthony's party.

She didn't have to wonder for very long.

"Be careful with that pin," said Mirror-Belle. "You don't want to prick your finger and end up asleep for a hundred years."

At that moment Ellen felt she would like nothing better. How *could* Mirror-Belle do this to her?

"Mirror-Belle, stay there! Don't come out of the mirror! You're not supposed to be here! Go back to Anthony's party!"

"No thank you very much." Mirror-Belle jumped down beside Ellen. She too held a safety pin and wore a baggy swimming costume with a broken shoulder strap. "I couldn't stand another game of Musical Thrones," she said.

"Don't you mean Musical Chairs?" asked Ellen.

"Yes, I think that *is* what they called it," said Mirror-Belle. "Musical Thrones is much better. You leap from throne to throne, and the thrones play tunes when you land on them."

"I hope you didn't leap about on the chairs?" said Ellen.

"I did try, but it was a bit hard because Tantrummy's mother kept taking them away."

"Anthony, not Tantrummy," Ellen corrected her, though Tantrummy did seem a better name for him. "Anyway, of course his mum took the chairs away – that's the whole point of Musical Chairs:

you take a chair away every time the music stops."

"Well, all that furniture-shifting seemed a lot of hard work for Tantrummy's mother," said Mirror-Belle. "She obviously needed some servants to help her. I can't think why she got so angry when I telephoned that removal firm."

Ellen gasped. "They didn't come, did they?"

"No – Tantrummy's mother cancelled them and made us play Keep the Parcel instead."

"Pass the Parcel, you mean."

"I can't remember exactly what they called it," said Mirror-Belle, "but it took me absolutely ages to unwrap the parcel – it was a terrible waste of so much wrapping

paper – and in the end there was only a tiny bag of sweets in the middle."

"But you're not supposed to unwrap the whole thing – you're just supposed to take off one wrapper and then pass it on."

"Don't be ridiculous, Ellen," said Mirror-Belle. "Didn't you know it's very rude to give away something which has been given to you?"

"I don't suppose Anthony was very pleased when you unwrapped the whole thing yourself."

"No, he started up a game of his own called Scream the House Down," said Mirror-Belle.

Ellen almost laughed, but then she remembered that she was the one who would be accused of all the things Mirror-Belle had done.

"I hope Auntie Pam didn't kick you out," she said.

"No – she summoned her magician," said Mirror-Belle.

"Oh, was there a conjuror? Was he good?"

"Unfortunately not. He just did a lot of tricks – not real magic at all. In the end I had to lend him a hand."

"How do you mean?"

"He offered to make one of us disappear," said Mirror-Belle. "He had a big long box and he asked Anthony to climb into it. Then he spun the box round a few times and opened a flap. We all looked into the box and it *did* look as though Anthony had disappeared. But then I lifted a different flap and there he was!"

"That was a bit mean to spoil the trick," said Ellen.

"Wait – I haven't finished," said Mirror-Belle. "I spotted that there was a mirror inside the empty part of the box – it made that space look bigger, which was why it looked as though Anthony had disappeared."

"I'm not sure if I understand," said Ellen.

"Never mind – I'm sure you'll understand the next bit," Mirror-Belle told her. "I climbed into the part of the box with the mirror in it and told the magician to close the lid, and then . . ."

"You disappeared through the mirror!" finished Ellen.

"Precisely. The magician must be delighted. At last it looks as if he's done some real magic!"

"I shouldn't think he's delighted at *all*! He's probably horrified," said Ellen, feeling horrified herself. "They must all be looking for me! I'll have to go back there – or else you will." Oh dear, which would be worse? To send Mirror-Belle back to Anthony's or to leave her in the swimming pool?

Just then Ellen heard voices. Livvy and the others were coming to get changed. Ellen ran and opened her locker, scooped out her clothes and dived into a changing cubicle. As she closed the door she heard Livvy greet Mirror-Belle:

"What took you so long, Ellen? It's time for the pizzas now. I'm going to have ham and pineapple."

"I'll have dragon and tomato," said Mirror-Belle, and Livvy laughed. Ellen changed quickly, and rubbed her hair as dry as she could. When she reckoned that all the others were in the cubicles she made her getaway. As she left the changing area she heard Livvy asking, "What's happened to your clothes, Ellen?" and Mirror-Belle replying, "I must have left them in the palace."

Instead of ringing Anthony's bell, Ellen crept round to the back door. It was unlocked and she tiptoed inside. She could hear voices calling her name upstairs; they must be searching the bedrooms. She peeped round the door of the sitting room. To her amazement the room was empty. On the floor was the long box which Mirror-Belle must have been talking about. Ellen lifted the lid and squeezed in. It was dark and cramped inside.

Almost immediately she heard the doorbell, followed by footsteps and voices in the hall.

"What do you mean, 'Just disappeared'?" This was her mother's voice.

"It's magic!" This was one of the children. "He's a really good conjuror. I want him to come to my party."

Then the conjuror: "It was nothing to do with me! I didn't even ask the wretched child to get into the box!"

"I want to see this box!" Mum's voice sounded really near now and Ellen realised that everyone had come into the sitting room.

"She's not there. We've looked hundreds of times," said Auntie Pam.

The next second the lid was opened and light streamed in.

"Ellen!" said Mum. Ellen climbed out and hugged her. Everyone clustered round.

"Fancy keeping her stuck in there all that time!" Mum accused the conjuror. "And why is her hair all damp?"

"I can't understand it!" he said. "This has never happened before."

Ellen felt sorry for him. She decided to tell the truth. "It's not his fault," she said. "It was Mirror-Belle."

"Who's Mirror-Belle?" asked one of the children.

"It's Ellen's imaginary friend," explained Mum.

"What an imagination she's got!" said Auntie Pam. "She was making up all sorts of extraordinary stories earlier on." But Mum didn't hear this, because Anthony had started to clamour, "Why didn't *I* disappear? *I* want to be invisible! It's not fair – I want another go!"

When Ellen and Mum got home, Luke was on the phone.

"It's all right, here she is," Ellen heard him say. "No, her clothes look fine – a bit crumpled maybe, that's all. Yes, I'm sure. Goodbye, then."

"Who was that?" asked Mum.

"This weird woman," said Luke. "Mrs Duck or someone."

"Was it Livvy Drake's mother?"

"Yes, Drake, that was it. She wanted to

know if Ellen was all right."

"Why shouldn't she be all right?" asked Mum.

"Don't ask me. I couldn't understand what the woman was on about. Something about Ellen's clothes getting stolen from the swimming pool."

"But Ellen wasn't at the swimming pool."

"That's what I told her, but she kept on about it. She said Ellen's locker was empty and there must have been a thief. She said they had to get some different clothes from Lost Property."

"She's obviously mixing Ellen up with some other child," said Mum.

"And then she said Ellen just disappeared when the rest of them were eating pizzas," went on Luke. "She was worried she might have been kidnapped."

"How strange," said Mum. She gave Ellen another hug. "I think you've had quite enough adventures for one day without being kidnapped, don't you?" she asked.

"Yes," said Ellen. "I certainly do."

Chapter Two

Wobblesday

Ellen hadn't seen Mirror-Belle for a few weeks. At the beginning of the summer holidays her family had moved house. The new house was in a different town, and Ellen had the feeling that Mirror-Belle had lost track of her. If so, she wasn't exactly sorry. Their adventures always seemed to end up with Ellen getting into trouble and Mirror-Belle escaping. Still, just sometimes Ellen found herself

looking in the mirror and half-hoping that her reflection would do something surprising. She would have liked someone to play with. There weren't any children in either of the houses next door. A girl of about her own age lived further down the street, but Ellen was too shy to say hello. She hoped she would make some friends when she started at her new school, but she felt quite nervous about that too.

When a fair came to the common near their new house, Mum said Ellen's big brother Luke could take her as long as he stayed with her. This sounded like fun, but the trouble was that Ellen and Luke wanted to do different things. Luke liked the kind of rides where you went flying and plunging about, preferably upside down and back to front. Ellen liked being scared too, but not in an upside-down sort of way. She wanted to go on the ghost train, but Luke said that was just for kids.

"I'll see you back here in an hour, OK?" said Luke. They were in the Wobbly Mirror Hall.

Ellen pretended to forget that Luke was supposed to stay with her.

"All right," she said. She wasn't looking at Luke but at herself in one of the wobbly mirrors. Her mouth was gaping like a cave in her droopy chin, above a long wiggly body and little waddly legs. "Look at me!"

she said, laughing and pointing, but Luke had already gone. Instead, it was the peculiar reflection who replied.

"Don't point, it's rude," she said, and stepped out of the mirror.

"Mirror-Belle, it's you!" said Ellen, and laughed again. "You've gone all funny and wobbly."

"Of course I'm wobbly, it's Wobblesday today, isn't it?"

"No, it's Wednesday," said Ellen.

"Call it that if you like," said Mirror-Belle, waddling out of the Mirror Hall on her short legs, "but where *I* come from it's a Wobblesday, and everyone wobbles on Wobblesdays. It's a rule my father the King made. Even the *palace* goes wobbly on Wobblesdays. A bit like that one," she added, pointing to a bouncy castle on which some children were jumping about. The finger Mirror-Belle was pointing with looked like a wiggly knitting needle and Ellen laughed again. She found she was really glad to see Mirror-Belle after all. She hadn't exactly been looking forward to going on the ghost train by herself.

"Have you got any money?" Ellen asked. Mirror-Belle had three 50p and two 20p pieces.

"Exactly the same as me," said Ellen. "But all the writing is back to front on your coins."

"It's *yours* that are the wrong way round, silly," said Mirror-Belle.

They each gave 50p to the man in charge of the ghost train, who was chewing gum and staring at nothing. He didn't seem to notice Mirror-Belle's strange appearance or the backwards writing.

They got into a carriage of the ghost train behind a woman and a little boy.

"It'll be fun travelling on an ordinary

train," said Mirror-Belle. "I've only ever been on a royal one before."

"This one isn't exactly *ordinary*—" Ellen warned, but was interrupted by an eerie voice:

"This is your Guaaaaaard speaking," the voice moaned. "Ride if you dare but prepare for a scare."

"What a silly guard!" said Mirror-Belle. "Why doesn't he tell us what stations we'll be going to and whether we can get tea

and snacks on the train?"

The train set off. Almost immediately it plunged into a tunnel. As they turned a corner a luminous monster popped out at them. The little boy in front screamed.

"This is disgraceful, frightening innocent children!" said Mirror-Belle. As she spoke, a huge spider dangled down from the ceiling and the boy screamed again.

"Don't they ever sweep their tunnels?" said Mirror-Belle.

She reached up and grabbed the spider with her long wiggly fingers.

"Go and build your web somewhere else," she said, throwing it over her shoulder. The people in the seats behind screamed.

The train turned another corner, where a ghost loomed out of the darkness and went "Whooo!" at the little boy. He clutched his mother.

"This is too bad," said Mirror-Belle. She leaned out of the carriage and went "Whooo!" back at the ghost, only much louder. The little boy turned round, saw Mirror-Belle and screamed again. Ellen wasn't surprised: with her gaping mouth and dangling chin Mirror-Belle probably looked like another ghost or monster to the little boy.

A few skeletons, vampires and coffins later the train stopped, and the little boy stopped screaming. "Can we have another go?" he said to his mother.

Mirror-Belle looked around her in disgust. "This is ridiculous," she said. "We haven't gone anywhere at all – we're back where we started. I'm going to complain to the stationmaster." She got out and headed towards the gum-chewing man, but Ellen managed to stop her.

"Why don't we have a go at the hoopla?" she said. "Look, we could win one of those giant teddies."

Ellen had never won a prize at hoopla. She could never manage to throw her hoop over a peg so that it landed flat, and

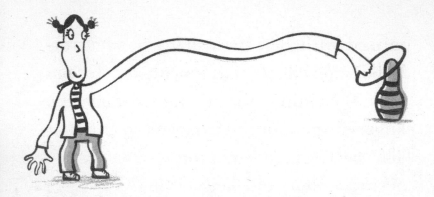

this time was no different. But for Mirror-
Belle it was easy. She just reached out one
of her amazingly long arms and put the
hoop over the peg. Soon she had won three
teddies and a goldfish in a bowl. A little
crowd had gathered around them.

"Here, you take these," said Mirror-
Belle, thrusting the teddies and goldfish
at Ellen and moving on to the coconut shy.
The crowd followed.

The man at the coconut shy looked
pleased to see so many people. Ellen

missed with her three balls but Mirror-Belle's long arm reached almost to the stands holding the coconuts and she knocked them out with no trouble. The crowd grew bigger and some of the people started having goes. The coconut man didn't seem to mind Mirror-Belle winning so often, and even gave her a sack to put the teddies and coconuts in.

"I think you'd better stop before it gets too heavy to carry," said Ellen. "Do you like candyfloss?"

"Wobbably," said Mirror-Belle.

"Don't you mean, 'probably'?"

"No, I mean *wobbably*. That means that if the candyfloss is wobbly I'll like it. You seem to have forgotten that this is Wobblesday. On Wobblesdays we only eat wobbly food."

It took some time to reach the candyfloss stall, as Mirror-Belle could only take tiny steps with her short legs, while her long body wobbled about all over the place.

Mirror-Belle asked for two wobbly candyflosses. The candyfloss seller gave her a funny look but she wiggled the sticks about a lot as she spun the pink stuff round them, and Mirror-Belle decided that would do. Her mouth was so huge that she ate hers in one mouthful and asked for five more. "I've got yards and yards of tummy to fill, you see," she said, after she'd eaten all five at once.

By now all their money was used up, and Ellen remembered she was supposed to be meeting Luke at the Mirror Hall. They went back there.

Outside the Mirror Hall there was a sign saying, "Wobbly Mirror-Hall, 20p."

"*Really!*" said Mirror-Belle. "As if it's not bad enough everything being in backwards writing, they can't even spell my name."

She took a felt-tip pen out of her pocket, changed two of the letters and added one. The sign now said, "Wobbly Mirror-Belle, 20p".

"Now, Ellen," she said, "you collect the money. Remember, it's twenty pence a wobble." She took up a position beside the notice, standing completely still, as if she was playing Musical Statues.

Ellen shuffled from foot to foot, not sure what to do. A few people gathered round.

"Twenty pence for what?" asked one.

"To see her wobble," said Ellen.

"She can't wobble, she's just a statue," said another.

"Isn't she that funny girl that was winning all the coconuts?" asked someone else.

In the end a man handed Ellen 20p, saying he wanted it back if he wasn't satisfied. As Ellen's palm closed round the coin, Mirror-Belle's body began to ripple, like a snake-charmer's snake rearing out of its basket and writhing about. She kept it up for half a minute and then stopped abruptly.

Immediately someone else gave Ellen 20p, and this time Mirror-Belle stretched out one of her long snaky arms. The crowd watched it wobble, curving and bending and eventually tying itself into a knot. Everyone clapped, except for one man who muttered, "It's all done with mirrors," in a knowing way.

The third time, Mirror-Belle wobbled her ears. They bounced up and down like yo-yos, nearly hitting the ground and then springing back up again. By this time the crowd was quite big, and everybody seemed to be reaching into their pockets.

Then Ellen noticed Luke strolling towards them from a ride called Jaws of Terror, his gelled hair glinting in the sunshine.

"Here comes my brother!" she said to Mirror-Belle.

With one last bounce of her ears Mirror-Belle turned and waddled, surprisingly quickly, into the Mirror Hall.

"Hey, you haven't paid!" the attendant called out.

50

"I'll pay for her," said Ellen. She gave the attendant two of the three 20ps they had earned, and followed Mirror-Belle, but she was overtaken by several of the crowd, eager for more wobbly stunts. Ellen looked around for Mirror-Belle but couldn't find her. Instead, she bumped into Luke.

"There you are!" he said. "You don't know what you've missed! That Space-Lurcher – it's amazing the way it stops and changes direction just when you're upside down at the top. You really feel you're going to fall out." Then he noticed the goldfish bowl and the sack. He looked inside the sack and saw the teddies and coconuts.

"Did you win all those?" he asked. Ellen could tell he was trying not to sound too impressed. She nearly said, "No, Mirror-Belle did," but she knew Luke wouldn't believe her. She guessed, too, that Mirror-Belle would by now have made her getaway into one of the wobbly mirrors. So instead she answered, "Yes – and I've still got twenty pence left!"

Chapter Three

Love-Potion Crisps

It was the first day of term and Ellen was starting at her new school. Mum took her to the head teacher's office, and the head teacher took her to her classroom.

"This is Ellen, who is going to be joining your class," she announced. All the other children stared at Ellen. She clutched her lunch box

tightly and tried to smile.

"Hello, Ellen," said the teacher brightly. "Perhaps you'd like to hang your blazer up in the cloakroom next door? You'll find a peg in there with your name on it."

Ellen found her peg and hung up her blazer. Underneath it she wore a tunic and blouse, and a tie with diagonal green and yellow stripes. Her old school didn't have a uniform, so she had never worn a tie before. She checked in the cloakroom mirror to make sure it was straight.

Yes, the tie looked fine but, oh dear, Ellen didn't feel like going back into the classroom and being stared at again.

She was just turning away from the mirror when a voice said, "You *do* look worried. Never fear, I'll be there."

Ellen turned back in time to see Mirror-Belle stepping cheerfully out of the mirror. She carried a lunch box just like Ellen's and was wearing the same uniform, except that the stripes in her tie sloped in the opposite direction.

"Mirror-Belle! *You* can't come to school with me!" said Ellen.

"What do you mean, I can't? I just have, haven't I?" said Mirror-Belle. She skipped past Ellen out of the cloakroom and opened the classroom door.

"Hello again, Ellen," said the teacher, and then looked surprised as she saw the real Ellen behind Mirror-Belle.

"I didn't know you had a twin," she said.

"Well, nevcr mind," said Mirror-Belle. "You can't know everything. I don't suppose

you know how many fairy godmothers I've
got either."

"Now, Ellen, don't be cheeky," said the
teacher.

"That's something else you don't know,"
said Mirror-Belle. "I'm not Ellen, I'm
Mirror-Belle."

"Very well, Mirror-Belle, now come and sit down at this table. You and Ellen can be in Orange group."

"I'd rather be in Gold group or Silver group," said Mirror-Belle.

"We don't have either of those, I'm afraid," said the teacher firmly, "but I'm sure you'll get on fine in Orange group if you behave yourself."

She gave out some exercise books and asked the children to write about what they had done in the holidays. Ellen wrote about moving house.

The teacher wandered round the classroom. She came over to Orange group's table and looked over Mirror-Belle's shoulder.

"Yours is a bit difficult to read, Mirror-Belle," she said. "Your letters seem to be the wrong way round. It is easy to get muddled up, I know, especially between 'b's and 'd's."

"Oh, poor you," said Mirror-Belle. "Do you really get as muddled up as all that? Don't worry – I'm sure you'll learn. Perhaps you'd better use a mirror to read my writing."

"That's quite a good idea," said the teacher, and took a mirror out of her handbag. "Yes, I can read it fine now. Mirror-Belle's written a very interesting story," she told the class. "Do you mind if I read it out, Mirror-Belle?"

"Not at all," said Mirror-Belle. "I expect you could do with a bit of reading practice."

The teacher read out Mirror-Belle's story. It went like this:

"I didn't do very much in the holidays because I got turned into a golden statue. You see, my father the King was nicc to an old man and so he was given the power to turn everything he touched to gold. By mistake he touched me. In the end I got turned back by being washed in a magic river."

The children all laughed at this story, and the teacher said, "That  was good, Mirror-Belle, although I seem to have heard that story before somewhere. What I asked you to write about was what you really did in the holidays."

"But I told you, I didn't do anything," said Mirror-Belle. "You can't when you're a golden statue – you can't move, or eat or brush your hair or anything. I had this awful tickle on my leg and I couldn't even scratch it."

At this point the bell for morning play rang. A friendly girl called Katy took Ellen and Mirror-Belle into the playground where they joined in a game of tig. But two big boys kept bumping into Ellen. They pretended it was by accident but Ellen could tell it was on purpose.

"That's Bruce Baxter and Stephen Hodge," said Katy. "They're *always* like that." Mirror-Belle said nothing but looked very thoughtful.

After playtime the teacher gave out some maths books and asked the children to turn to a page which had a picture of a fruit shop.

"Now," she said, "if one apple costs ten pence and Susan gives the fruit-seller fifty pence, how much change will she get?"

"Hold on a second," said Mirror-Belle. "Look at those apples. Would you say they're half red and half green?"

"What about it, Mirror-Belle?"

"I think Susan ought to watch out," said Mirror-Belle. "How does she know the apple-selling lady hasn't poisoned the apples? She's probably a wicked queen in disguise, trying to get rid of anyone more beautiful than her."

"*Mirror-Belle!*" said the teacher angrily. "I'm not asking you to tell fairy stories. I asked how much *change* Susan would get from her fifty pence. How much do you think?"

"None," said Mirror-Belle. "If that queen's as wicked as I think she is, she'll run off with the fifty pence."

By the time the bell rang for lunch the teacher was looking quite exhausted.

In the dinner hall Ellen and Mirror-Belle sat with Katy and the other children who had brought packed lunches. Unfortunately, these included Bruce Baxter and Stephen Hodge. When the dinner lady wasn't looking Bruce grabbed Ellen's bag of crisps. Then Stephen took Katy's chocolate  bar and Bruce snatched another child's yogurt. They put all the things in a bag along with some other goodies they had stolen.

"They always do that," said Katy. "Then they eat them in the playground."

"But why don't you tell the dinner lady?" asked Ellen.

"If you do that they lie in wait on the way home from school and pounce on you."

Once again Mirror-Belle was being unusually quiet and thoughtful. She had managed to avoid having her lunch stolen, and she took an unopened packet of crisps out into the playground. They looked just like Ellen's crisps except for the writing being back to front.

Katy and her friends had a long skipping rope and they asked Ellen and Mirror-Belle to play with them. But Bruce Baxter and Stephen Hodge kept barging into the game and treading on the rope. Stephen was swinging the bag of stolen food. Just as they were interrupting the game for the fourth time, Mirror-Belle said loudly, "I see I've got love-potion-flavoured crisps today."

"What are they?" said Ellen.

"They make you fall in love with the first person you see."

She popped one into her mouth, fixing

her eyes on Bruce
Baxter.

"Oh, my hero!"
she suddenly
exclaimed. Then she
ran up to him and
hugged him. Bruce
went red. All the girls laughed at him and
so did Stephen.

"Let me shower you with kisses!" said
Mirror-Belle, aiming a kiss at Bruce's
nose. He turned away and the kiss landed
on his ear.

"You were so wonderful when you were
spoiling the skipping game," she said.
"*Please* do it again and I'll give you *ten*
kisses!"

"Leave me alone," said Bruce.

"Never!" cried Mirror-Belle. She bit into another crisp, at the same time staring at Stephen Hodge. "Oh, my darling!" she said. "My own true love!" She threw her arms around Stephen and this time it was his turn to go red.

"You're so *clever* to have taken all that food. You *won't* give it back, will you?"

"Come on, let's go!" said Stephen to Bruce, looking very embarrassed.

"Where you go I follow!" said Mirror-Belle. "The only way to break the spell is to give me a bag of food, but I'm sure you won't want to do that, will you?"

The boys dumped the bag at Mirror-Belle's feet and ran off.

After Mirror-Belle had given the food back to its owners the skipping game started up again, this time undisturbed.

"Are those *really* magic crisps?" asked Katy.

"Try one and see!" said Mirror-Belle.

Katy ate a crisp and so did Ellen, but

neither of them fell in love with anyone.

"Perhaps it only works on princesses," said Mirror-Belle.

Back in the classroom the teacher got the paints out and told the children to roll up their sleeves and put aprons on.

"We're going to do a project on pets this term," she said. "I'd like you all to paint a picture of a pet. It can either be your own pet or one belonging to a friend."

Ellen started on a picture of her goldfish. The teacher came over to their table.

"That's good, Ellen," she said. "I like those wiggly water weeds." She looked at Mirror-

Belle's paper. "I see you're painting two animals, Mirror-Belle. What are they? A dog and a cat?"

"No," said Mirror-Belle, "a lion and a unicorn."

"What an imagination you've got!" said the teacher.

"It's not me who's got the imagination, it's them!" said Mirror-Belle. "For some reason they both seem to imagine they should be sitting on the throne instead of my father. They're always fighting for the crown. It's a wonder they haven't torn each other to pieces by now."

But the teacher had stopped listening and was looking instead at Mirror-Belle's hands and arms. They were covered in yellow splodges.

"You've got an awful lot of paint on yourself, Mirror-Belle," she said.

"Oh dear me," said Mirror-Belle. "That's not paint – I think I'm turning into gold again! I thought I was feeling a bit peculiar. I'll have to have a dip in that magic river before I get solid."

"I'm sure you'll find the tap water in the cloakroom will do the job, Mirror-Belle," the teacher said sternly. "And if you're still feeling peculiar after that you can go to the medical room."

"How could I get there if I've turned to gold?" asked Mirror-Belle, as she left the classroom.

Ten minutes later, when she still hadn't come back, the teacher sent Ellen into the cloakroom. Ellen wasn't surprised at what she found. Mirror-Belle had gone, and the cloakroom mirror was covered in smears of yellow paint. On the floor Ellen found a scrap of paper with some backwards writing on it. She held it up to the mirror and read:

Dear Ellen, Sorry I had to go. Love Mirror-Belle. P.S. Give Bruce Baxter and Stephen Hodge a kiss each from me.

Mirror-Belle never came back to school. The head teacher wrote a letter to Ellen's mum saying, *You only enrolled one child at our school, and we feel that your other child might fit in better somewhere else.* Ellen's mum thought this was rather strange.

"I wasn't thinking of sending Luke to

Ellen's school – he's too old, in any case," she said.

Ellen made some friends at school and soon stopped feeling shy. But she never gave Bruce or Stephen their kiss from Mirror-Belle because they didn't come anywhere near her.

Bruce and Stephen weren't taking any chances. The new girl looked normal.  As far as they could tell her crisps were normal. She said she was called Ellen. But maybe – just maybe – she was really Mirror-Belle.

★ JULIA DONALDSON ★

Princess Mirror-Belle

and the Magic Shoes

Turn the page to read an extract . . .

Illustrated by

✳ LYDIA MONKS ✳

Chapter One

The Magic Shoes

"Hey, you! Yes, you! Turn around, look over your shoulder," sang Ellen's brother, Luke, into the microphone.

Ellen was sitting in the village hall watching Luke's band, Breakneck, rehearse for the Battle of the Bands. The hall was nearly empty, but that evening it would be packed with fans of the six different bands who were entering the competition.

As well as being Breakneck's singer,

Luke wrote most of their songs, including this one.

"It's me! Yes, me! Turn around, I'm still here," he sang. Then he wandered moodily around the stage, while the lead guitarist, Steph, played a twangy solo.

Steph, who never smiled, wore frayed baggy black trousers with a pointless chain hanging out of the pocket and a black T-shirt with orange flames on it. The solo went on and on.

"Steph's so good at the guitar," Ellen whispered to Steph's sister Seraphina, who was sitting next to her.

"I know," said Seraphina. She was two years older than Ellen and dressed very much like her brother, except that her T-shirt had a silver skull on it. "But I bet they don't win. I don't think they should have chosen this song. It's not going to get people dancing. Steph wrote a much better one called 'Savage'."

Ellen couldn't imagine Steph writing anything dancy, but she was quite shy of Seraphina and didn't say so. Besides, she had just remembered something.

"Dancing – help! I'm going to be late for ballet!" She picked up a bag from the floor.

"You've got the wrong bag – that's mine," said Seraphina, who also went to ballet, but to a later class.

"Sorry." Ellen grabbed her own bag and hurried to the door.

At least she didn't have far to go. The ballet classes were held in a room called

the studio, which was above the hall. Ellen ran up the stairs.

The changing room was empty. The other girls must be in the studio already, but Ellen couldn't hear any music so the class couldn't have started yet.

Hurriedly, she put on her leotard and

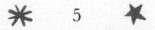

ballet shoes and scooped her hair into the hairnet that Madame Jolie, the ballet teacher, insisted they all wear. Madame Jolie was very fussy about how they looked and could pounce on a girl for the smallest thing, such as crossing the ribbons on her ballet shoes in the wrong way.

Ellen was just giving herself a quick check in the full-length mirror when a voice said, "What's happened to your feet?"

It was a voice that she knew very well. It was coming from the mirror and it belonged to Princess Mirror-Belle.

About the Author and Illustrator

Julia Donaldson is one of the UK's most popular children's writers. Her award-winning books include *What the Ladybird Heard, The Snail and the Whale* and *The Gruffalo*. She has also written many children's plays and songs, and her sell-out shows based on her books and songs are a huge success. She was the Children's Laureate from 2011 to 2013, campaigning for libraries and for deaf children, and creating a website for teachers called picturebookplays.co.uk. Julia and her husband Malcolm divide their time between Sussex and Edinburgh. You can find out more about Julia at www.juliadonaldson.co.uk.

Lydia Monks studied Illustration at Kingston University, graduating in 1994 with a first-class degree. She is a former winner of the Smarties Bronze Award for *I Wish I Were a Dog* and has illustrated many books by Julia Donaldson. Her illustrations have been widely admired.

Also available

JULIA DONALDSON

Princess Mirror-Belle

THREE STORIES IN ONE

Illustrated by
LYDIA MONKS

For younger readers

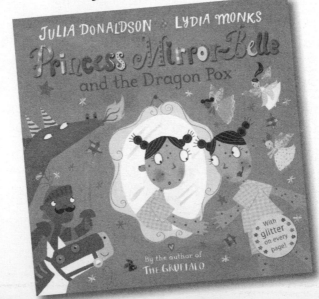

JULIA DONALDSON · LYDIA MONKS

Princess Mirror-Belle
and the Dragon Pox

With glitter on every page!

By the author of
THE GRUFFALO